T0193578

The big banana

made by
Liam Frew

THE BIG BANANA
A Lion Cub's Adventures Season 1, episode 2:

Copyright © 2020 Liam Frew.

iUniverse books may be ordered through booksellers or by contacting:

iUniverse
1663 Liberty Drive
Bloomington, IN 47403
www.iuniverse.com
844-349-9409

Because of the dynamic nature of the Internet, any web addresses or links contained in this book may have changed since publication and may no longer be valid. The views expressed in this work are solely those of the author and do not necessarily reflect the views of the publisher, and the publisher hereby disclaims any responsibility for them.

ISBN: 978-1-6632-0454-7 (sc)
ISBN: 978-1-6632-0455-4 (e)

Library of Congress Control Number: 2020913217

Print information available on the last page.

iUniverse rev. date: 08/06/2020

Table of contents

chapter 1. the early wake up

chapter 3. the big banana

let me explain Lion cub...

raccoon: every year the wildebeest travel to the big banana...It was named after it's size...the reason why they eat it.. is because it's actually good for the banana..because If it doesn't get eatin' in a year...it will turn to dust ...and it will never grow again

Chapter 4. On the move

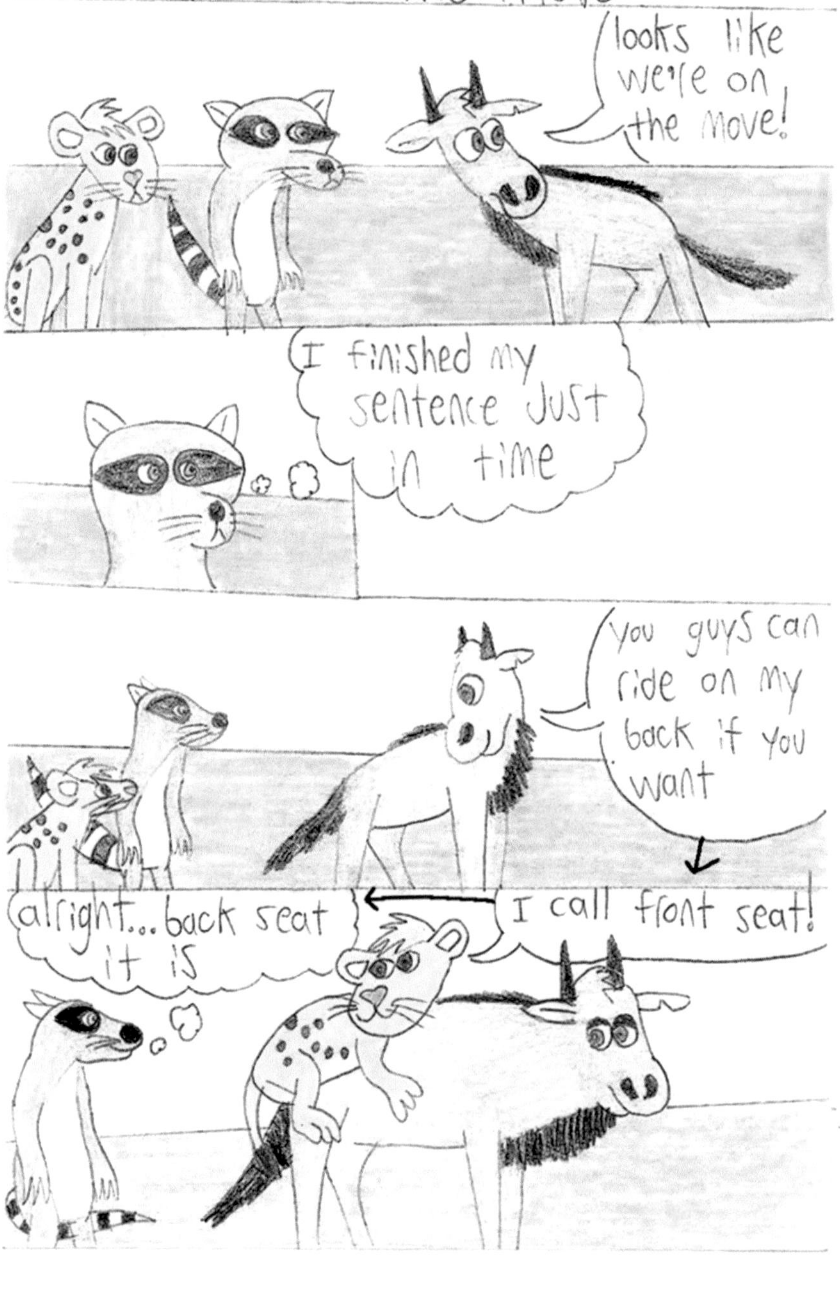

Chapter 5. prehistoric death zone

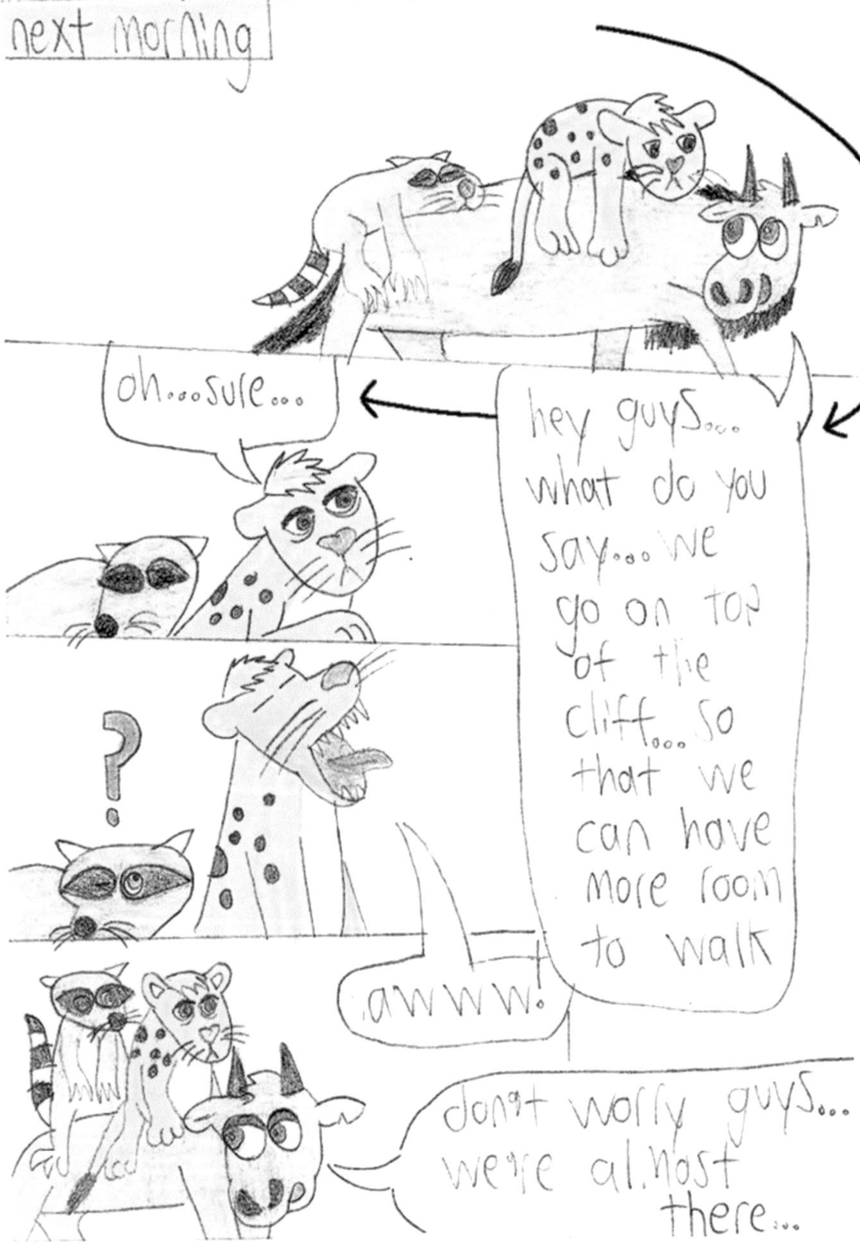

meanwhile back in the prehistoric canyon
we're surrounded!
make that six of them
Grr!
roar!
Lion cub!
tigress!

2 minutes later after tigress kicked the herrerasaurus butt

chapter 6. the end

you stupid Lion!...did you follow us all the way out here?!

nevermind that!... I've come to claim my prize...the Lion cub...now get out of my sight or else...

Printed in the United States
By Bookmasters